Dear Parents,

Welcome to the Scholastic Reader series. We have taken over 80 years of experience with teachers, parents, and children and put it into a program that is designed to match your child's interests and skills.

Level 1—Short sentences and stories made up of words kids can sound out using their phonics skills and words that are important to remember.

Level 2—Longer sentences and stories with words kids need to know and new "big" words that they will want to know.

Level 3—From sentences to paragraphs to longer stories, these books have large "chunks" of texts and are made up of a rich vocabulary.

Level 4—First chapter books with more words and fewer pictures.

It is important that children learn to read well enough to succeed in school and beyond. Here are ideas for reading this book with your child:

- Look at the book together. Encourage your child to read the title and make a prediction about the story.
- Read the book together. Encourage your child to sound out words when appropriate. When your child struggles, you can help by providing the word.
- Encourage your child to retell the story. This is a great way to check for comprehension.
- Have your child take the fluency test on the last page to check progress.

Scholastic Readers are designed to support your child's efforts to learn how to read at every age and every stage. Enjoy helping your child learn to read and love to read.

—**Francie Alexander**
Chief Education Officer
Scholastic Education

For Rebecca
—G.H.

For Julianna,
who's an artist too
—P.B.F.

Library of Congress Cataloging-in-Publication Data is available.

ISBN 0-439-09907-2

15 14 13 12 09 10 11 12

Printed in the U.S.A. 23
First printing, December 1999

Slip! Slide! Skate!

by Gail Herman
Illustrated by Paige Billin-Frye

Scholastic Reader — Level 2

SCHOLASTIC INC.
New York Toronto London Auckland Sydney
Mexico City New Delhi Hong Kong Buenos Aires

"I have a surprise for you,"
Mom tells me.
"Ice skates!"
My first pair!
Soon I will be the best
ice-skater on my block.

Mom takes me for lessons.

Annie, the teacher, shows us how to lace our skates.

Easy! I think.

Then we all stand up.
My feet feel wobbly.

Oops! I sit down.
"Do you need help?"
asks Annie.

"No thanks," I answer.

"I need help!" says Beth.

Annie takes us onto the ice.

I stumble a bit.

But we all hold the railing.

"Now let go!" Annie calls.
"And glide if you can!"
"Of course I can,"
I whisper.
"I'm going to be the best!"

I move slowly.
But I am doing it.
I am gliding!

"Ow!"
Beth falls down next to me.
Annie and I help her up.
Beth giggles
and falls down again.
"This is fun," she says.

Falling down is fun?
I shake my head.
Beth will never be the best.

Weeks go by,
and now I skate
even better.

I slide and glide
and zoom and zip.

I am the best skater
in our whole class!

"Next week we will be in
the Ice Show,"
Annie tells us.
"You will skate in a line,
holding hands."

That is too easy, I think.
Beth laughs and claps her hands.
"That sounds like fun!" she says.
I look at her and frown.
"We are not here to have fun,"
I say.
"We are here to put on a show!"

We practice holding hands
and skating.
I am getting bored.
I want to slide and glide
and zoom and zip.
So everyone knows
I am the best!

Then it is the day of the Ice Show.
I watch the other skaters.
They are so pretty.
They move like ballerinas.

Now it is our turn.
I am in the lead.
I hold Beth's hand.
Beth holds Lisa's hand.
Lisa holds Jack's hand.
Jack holds Ben's hand.
We glide in a straight line.
I know we look nice.
But those other skaters?
They are the best.
Unless . . .

We go faster!
I speed up.
Beth speeds up.

So do Lisa and Jack
and Ben.
Now we are moving!

I do not notice a bump in the ice.
I trip over the bump,
and fall—*splat*—on the ground.
I pull down Beth.
Beth pulls down Lisa.
Lisa pulls down Jack.
And Jack pulls down Ben.

Oh, no!
I have ruined the show!

Then Beth laughs.
Lisa and Jack and Ben laugh, too.
Everyone is laughing.
All at once, I giggle.
I try to stand up.
But I fall down again.
Now I laugh harder.

I am not the best,

I think.

But this is a lot more fun!